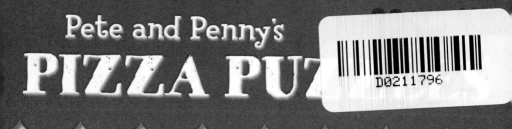

Pete and Penny's
PIZZA PUZZLES

Case of the Bookstore Burglar

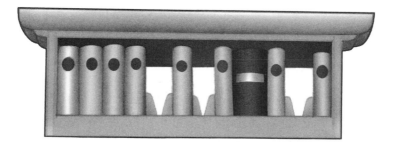

by Aaron Rosenberg
illustrated by David Harrington

PSS!
PRICE STERN SLOAN
An Imprint of Penguin Group (USA) Inc.

For Adara and Arthur, who always come first in my book
and in my heart. Even before pizza—AR

For my awesome nephews, Ben and Charlie—DH

PRICE STERN SLOAN
Published by the Penguin Group
Penguin Group (USA) Inc., 375 Hudson Street, New York, New York 10014, USA
Penguin Group (Canada), 90 Eglinton Avenue East, Suite 700,
Toronto, Ontario M4P 2Y3, Canada
(a division of Pearson Penguin Canada Inc.)
Penguin Books Ltd., 80 Strand, London WC2R 0RL, England
Penguin Group Ireland, 25 St. Stephen's Green, Dublin 2, Ireland
(a division of Penguin Books Ltd.)
Penguin Group (Australia), 250 Camberwell Road, Camberwell,
Victoria 3124, Australia
(a division of Pearson Australia Group Pty. Ltd.)
Penguin Books India Pvt. Ltd., 11 Community Centre,
Panchsheel Park, New Delhi—110 017, India
Penguin Group (NZ), 67 Apollo Drive, Rosedale, Auckland 0632, New Zealand
(a division of Pearson New Zealand Ltd.)
Penguin Books (South Africa) (Pty.) Ltd., 24 Sturdee Avenue,
Rosebank, Johannesburg 2196, South Africa

Penguin Books Ltd., Registered Offices:
80 Strand, London WC2R 0RL, England

ISBN 978-0-8431-9809-6   10 9 8 7 6 5 4 3 2 1

Chapter One

"Whoa, where is that noise coming from?" Penny Pizzarelli asked. She jumped down the last few stairs into the kitchen. Her younger brother, Pete, was right behind her. For once, *they* weren't the ones being loud!

"It sounds like a herd of elephants!" Pete said. "And our restaurant's not even open right now!" Pizzarelli's Pizza Parlor was always closed between lunch and dinner. And Sunday dinner was a few hours away.

"There's a new store going in next door," said Mrs. Pizzarelli. She spread the secret Pizzarelli sauce onto a pizza. Today's lunch rush had been so busy, the family hadn't had time to eat.

"Really? Somebody finally bought that place?" asked Penny. She was tall and blond like their mom. Pete had dark hair and was stocky like their dad.

"Yes, it's going to be a bookstore," Mr. Pizzarelli said. "The grand opening is Friday night. But the owner hopes to start selling books tomorrow."

"Wow, that's soon!" Pete said. He watched his father add cheese to the pizza. Pete loved to watch his parents work together. And he loved to eat their pizzas! Pizza was one of Pete's favorite things. Puzzles were the other.

"Yes, it's a big job to get a store ready that quickly," Mrs. Pizzarelli agreed. She reached above one of the cabinets for a fresh package of napkins. "But some of our neighbors are helping out. That's probably why there's so much noise."

"That and the brick wall between the two shops is old and crumbling," their dad added. He tossed pepperoni, olives, and mushrooms onto the pizza. Then he used the long, wooden handle to slide the pizza into the oven. A few minutes later the timer dinged and he pulled out the piping hot pizza.

"Oh, geez," Mr. Pizzarelli said, scratching his head as he set the pizza on the counter.

"I guess I wasn't watching what I was doing. The toppings aren't spread out evenly enough. How can we divide this pie into four slices so that each slice has the same number of pepperoni, mushrooms, and olives?"

Pete laughed. Mr. Pizzarelli was a pizza-making expert! He hadn't put the toppings on that way by mistake. He was giving Pete and Penny one of his special pizza puzzles!

Using only two straight lines, divide the pizza into four slices—with an equal number of each topping on each slice.

(Answer, page 62.)

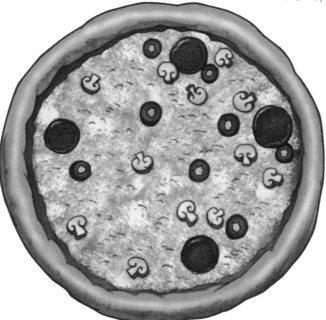

Pete and Penny tried to decide where to cut the pie. Pete picked up two breadsticks. Penny took one and laid it on top of the pizza to show where to cut. Pete studied what she'd done. Then he laid down the second breadstick. "Follow the breadsticks," he told his dad.

Mr. Pizzarelli smiled. "Nice work!" He cut along the breadsticks. Some slices were bigger than others. But now they each had a slice with the same number of pepperoni, mushrooms, and olives.

After they ate, Mr. Pizzarelli stood up. "I think I'll go meet our new neighbors," he said. "Anyone want to join me?"

"I'll come!" Penny said. She wiped her hands on a napkin. Then she hopped down from her stool.

"Me too!" Pete agreed.

"I'll stay here and get things ready for the dinner crowd," their mother said. "You three go ahead."

"We'll be back soon to help out," Mr. Pizzarelli promised. The bell chimed as the three of them walked outside.

The sign over the new shop next door said Tidy Tomes. Pete and Penny peeked in the window. The front window display was filled with tidy stacks of books. *Clearly this store owner takes organization very seriously*, thought Penny. Inside, the lights were on, and people were moving about. They saw several Redville residents.

"Hello!" Mr. Pizzarelli called out as they walked in. "Anybody seen the owner?"

A tall, thin man stepped out from behind the counter. His hair was very neat. "We aren't open until tomorrow," he explained, pushing his small, square glasses up on his nose.

"I know—we just wanted to introduce ourselves. We're your neighbors—the Pizzarellis," Mr. Pizzarelli replied.

"Oh. Well then, it's nice to meet you. I'm Theodore Tome," Mr. Tome said, reaching out to shake Mr. Pizzarelli's hand. "And that's my son, Jake, over there." He pointed across the shop to a tall, thin boy around Penny's age unpacking a box of books. "Jake, come and say hello." Jake waved but stayed where he was. *I guess he's too busy to say hi,* thought Penny. *Or maybe he's just not very friendly.*

"These are my children, Pete and Penny," said Mr. Pizzarelli. "When you get a chance, please come over to our pizza parlor for a bite."

"Jake and I definitely will," Mr. Tome promised. "Right now, we're just too busy."

Pete and Penny looked around. There were so many books! Bookshelves covered every wall. More shelves stood in intersecting rows, dividing the big store into smaller spaces. A few spots held chairs for reading. The shelves hid them from view, though. *It's like one big maze!* thought Pete.

"This is so exciting!" Penny said.

"Oh?" Mr. Tome studied her. "Do you like to read?"

"I love to!" Penny answered.

That got a smile out of him. "Well then, I hope to see you in here often."

"Hello, Pizzarellis!" Mr. Shears called out. He was the town barber, and he loved to tell stories. "This is just like when I helped set up a sardine store, back in 19—"

"Hi, Penny!" Ms. Green said, interrupting Mr. Shears. She owned Redville's grocery store, Vera's Veggies. "I hope you and your brother are eating enough greens!" She always worried that the Pizzarellis ate too much pizza. Pete and Penny didn't think that was possible!

Whoosh! Something flew down past Pete's ear. Then it bounced back up. Pete turned. There was a trampoline on the floor. A tall, bald man was standing up high on a ladder beside the trampoline. He was putting a book on a nearby shelf. A tall man with curly, red hair stood next to the trampoline holding a book. He was getting ready to jump back onto it. Both men wore brightly colored shirts, pants, and bow ties.

Pete laughed. It was the Jests, of course. They owned the local toy store, Jest Joking. They were grown men, but they acted like big kids.

"Hi, Elliot and Rupert!" Pete called out.

"Looks like you've figured out how to reach the high shelves!" Penny said with a smile.

Just then, a big, bearded figure entered the store. "Oh hello, young Pizzarellis," he said.

"Hi, Mr. Fields!" Pete and Penny replied. Mr. Fields was their science teacher. He lived in a small house with a huge backyard and grew all kinds of flowers and vegetables.

"I wanted to stop by while I could," Mr. Fields announced, lifting a box of books. "I'm going to be ridiculously busy the rest of the week—I'm preparing for the big Tastiest Tomato competition next weekend. It's my first time entering. I want to make sure I'm ready."

"You'll do great," Penny assured him. Everyone knew that Mr. Fields grew amazing vegetables. Apparently he never shopped at Vera's Veggies. Mrs. Crier claimed this was because he thought his vegetables were better than anything Ms. Green sold. Mrs. Crier

owned the beauty salon in Redville. She was also the town gossip.

"Good luck," Mr. Pizzarelli added. "Speaking of busy, we need to get back to our shop to help prepare for the dinner crowd. Welcome to the neighborhood, though!"

"Thank you," Mr. Tome said. "Come back tomorrow to check out our selection!"

Pete and Penny walked toward the door with their dad.

"I'm surprised to see Mr. Fields here," Penny overheard Mrs. Crier telling Mr. Shears as they left. "Did you know he once wanted to buy this place himself? He planned to open his own vegetable shop to steal business from Vera! I hear he—"

The door shut. Penny was glad. *It isn't nice to gossip!* she thought.

Still, she couldn't help wondering what Mrs. Crier had been about to say. *What else had Mrs. Crier heard about Mr. Fields?*

Chapter Two

"See ya!" Pete's friend Steve shouted.

Steve lived two blocks away from the Pizzarelli's shop, so they had all walked home together after school the next day.

"Bye," Penny called after him.

Pete waved. Then he and Penny ran for the pizza parlor. They raced to see who could reach the door first.

"Ha!" Penny shouted as she unlocked the door. Pete followed her inside, shoulders hunched.

A flash of white on the floor caught Pete's eye as they stepped inside. "What's this?" He bent down. *It must have been slipped under the door.* He picked it up.

"What did you find?" Penny turned back toward him.

"An envelope," he answered. "And it has

our names on it!" Sure enough, *Pete and Penny* was scribbled on the front.

"What's inside?" Penny asked. "Let me see!" She snatched the envelope from Pete's hand.

He rolled his eyes and thought, *She's so impatient!*

Penny opened the envelope and pulled out a piece of paper. A series of letters had been printed on one side.

"It's a code!" Pete said. Penny handed over the paper so Pete could take a closer look. He loved puzzles and riddles and codes of all kinds.

Penny nodded. She loved puzzles almost as much as her brother did. "But how do we solve it?" she asked. "There isn't a key."

Pete frowned. Without a key, they wouldn't know what to replace each letter with. He studied the paper. "Well, the second word here only has three letters," he pointed out. "What's the most common three-letter word?"

"*The*," Penny said immediately.

"Okay, so what if that word is supposed to be *the*?" Pete asked.

Penny nodded. "That would mean *u* equals *t*, *i* equals *h*, and *f* equals *e*."

Pete grinned. "Each letter in the coded
message must stand for the letter before it in the
alphabet! That must be the key!" He pulled out
a pencil. They sat down in a booth and started
replacing each letter with the one before it in the
alphabet.

Decode the message.

(Answer, page 62.)

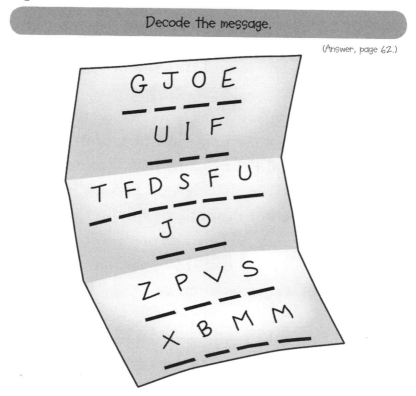

Penny read the message aloud. "What does
that mean?"

Before Pete could answer, the shop door opened. He tucked the paper into his back pocket. "Hello!" It was Benny Grande. "I hope I'm not too early for dinner!" Benny owned the town coffee shop, Benny's Beans.

"No, you're right on time!" Mrs. Pizzarelli answered as she came out of the kitchen. "We'll have your slices ready in a jiffy! Hey, kids, how about putting your school things away? Then you can help out."

"Okay," Penny said. She and Pete went upstairs to drop their backpacks in their bedrooms.

When Pete and Penny came back downstairs, half the booths were already full. Pizzarelli's was a favorite restaurant of many people in town. But Pete and Penny wished the place were empty tonight. They wanted to investigate what "Find the secret in your wall" could mean!

"Would you like anything else today?" Pete asked Benny a bit later. He was tapping his pen on his notebook.

Benny laughed. "I'm not even done with the slices I have in front of me!" he replied. "Where's the fire, Pete? Afraid I'll eat all the pizza if I stay too long?"

Pete laughed. But he kept looking toward the wall. *What is that message trying to tell us?* thought Pete.

"Not a chance!" Rupert announced from the next booth over. "We'll eat it first!"

"It sure is busy for a Monday night," Elliot said. Penny had just brought him and Rupert their bill. "Maybe Mr. Tome is telling his customers to come here after they visit his store!"

"I doubt it," Mrs. Crier argued from her seat nearby. "Mr. Tome doesn't strike me as the kind to do anybody any favors. We all worked like dogs yesterday, and he didn't even offer us a discount."

Pete and Penny didn't say anything. They'd only met Mr. Tome for a few minutes. *He hadn't been very cheerful, but he seemed friendly enough considering how stressed he must have been about opening his new shop*, thought Penny.

It took a while, but finally everyone had left. Mr. Pizzarelli locked the door and flipped the sign to CLOSED. Penny swept the floors, while Pete emptied the trash.

"Okay," Penny said to Pete as soon as they finished their chores. "Time to figure out what this message means!"

Pete nodded and sank into a booth. "'Find the secret in your wall.' Hmmm . . ." He looked around the restaurant. "It could mean the brick wall between us and the bookstore."

"That would make sense. The message did show up on the same day the bookstore opened," said Penny. They ran their hands along the wall, but found nothing. Penny crossed her arms and leaned against it. Pete could tell she was about to complain. Instead, she almost fell over. "Something moved!" she whispered loudly.

Penny felt along where she'd been leaning. She found a loose brick! Pete examined the brick. He managed to pry it out with his pen. There was a space behind the brick, then another brick behind that one. They could see light leaking in around the edges.

"It's a hole through the wall!" Pete said softly. "Dad was right about these old walls. It's no wonder we can hear noise from next door!"

"Look at this!" Penny pulled a piece of paper out of the space between the two sides. The paper had a series of dots and short lines on it, all in neat rows. "What is this weird drawing?"

Pete shook his head. "It's some kind of code. But it's not any code I've seen before."

"Bedtime, you two!" Mrs. Pizzarelli called.

"Coming!" Penny called back. She slid the brick back into place. "We should stop by the bookstore tomorrow after school," she suggested. "Maybe they'll have a book about codes, so we can find out how to decode this one."

Pete nodded. "Good thinking! And maybe we'll figure out who left this in the wall in the first place," he said. "It must've been someone who was in the bookstore."

"—or someone who was in here," Penny added. She folded the paper and stuck it in her pocket. Then she and Pete headed up to bed.

Chapter Three

"Wow, this place looks great!" Pete said as he and Penny entered Tidy Tomes after school the next day. On Sunday night the bookstore had been filled with boxes. Now all the books were neatly organized on the bookshelves. People were browsing and chatting and reading. The store's grand opening celebration wasn't until Friday, but with customers bustling about, it looked like the store was already a success.

"Hi, kids!" Ms. Green said as she hurried past. They waved hello, but she'd already scooted out the door. *What's the big rush?* Pete wondered. Then he noticed Mr. Fields up by the register. *Had Ms. Green been avoiding Mr. Fields?*

"Look, there's Jake, the owner's son," Penny said to Pete. She waved, but Jake didn't seem to notice. His dad was talking to him.

"Look at that bookcase!" Mr. Tome said,

pointing across the shop. Pete and Penny looked where he was pointing. The bookcase was completely empty. It didn't even have shelves! Then they looked down at the floor. The shelves had all collapsed! A pile of books surrounded the bookcase.

"Why did you overstock that shelf?" Mr. Tome asked Jake. "You know the shelves can't handle that much weight. Plus, I found *this* over there!" He held up a book. "*Successful Soil Secrets*? You're supposed to alphabetize by section, Jake. This book shouldn't have been anywhere near that poetry bookcase!"

"Come on," Pete told Penny, pulling her away. "We shouldn't stare."

"If Mr. Tome doesn't want people staring, he shouldn't yell at Jake in the middle of his store," Penny muttered. She felt bad for Jake. He seemed shy, and being yelled at by his dad probably wasn't helping.

Pete found the Puzzles & Games section of the bookstore. He and Penny started looking through the books there. They recognized some of the books, but many were new to them.

"Hey, what's this?" Penny asked. She held up a book with the words *Morse code* on the cover.

"Those markings look just like the code in the message!" Pete took the book from her. "The message must be in Morse code!"

Mr. Tome was back at the counter when they brought the book up. Penny didn't see Jake anywhere. She still wanted to meet him.

"Ah, a book about Morse code," Mr. Tome said. "Jake said he'd heard something about you two liking puzzles and codes."

"He was right," Penny said. "We love puzzles. We've even been in the paper for solving mysteries with puzzles—twice!"

"That's quite impressive," replied Mr. Tome.

Pete and Penny paid for the book and then hurried home to solve the coded message.

"You have the paper with you, right?" Pete asked as soon as they were in the pizza parlor. He sat down at the nearest booth.

"Right here." Penny pulled the coded message out of her pocket. She sat down next to her brother.

Pete had already found the Morse code key in the front of their new book. Penny called out each set of dots and dashes. Pete told her what the dots and dashes equaled. Then Penny wrote each letter down.

Decode the message. (Use the secret code in the front of this book!)

(Answer, page 62.)

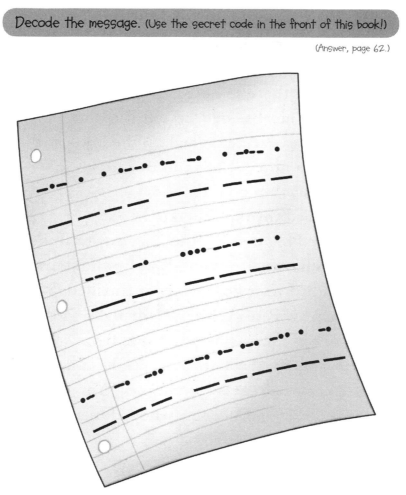

"Huh?" Penny shook her head. "We don't even have a garden!"

"Maybe this has something to do with Mr. Fields?" Pete suggested. "He *does* have the best garden around."

Penny shrugged. "I think we should go back to the bookstore before it closes," she said. "The first message came from over there. So maybe there's a clue there to help us figure out what this message means—or who left it for us."

"Good idea." Pete picked up the book and pocketed the note. "Let's put this new book upstairs first, though."

They raced through the kitchen.

"We need to go next door," Penny told their mother. She was already halfway up the stairs.

"Not until your homework is finished," their mom warned. Pete groaned. Normally he did his homework as soon as he got home from school. But he wanted to look for clues right away!

Pete knew better than to argue. "Yes, Mom," he replied. Pete and Penny trudged upstairs and got out their homework.

It was almost dinnertime when they finished. "Don't be out long," their dad said as Pete and Penny leaped down the stairs. "You won't need to help out here tonight, but it *is* a school night."

"We'll be back soon," Penny promised.

The mailman, Mr. Parcel, was just coming in as they neared the door. "Hello, Pizzarellis!" he called.

"Hi, Mr. Parcel!" He was always friendly. And he often brought Pete and Penny riddles to solve.

"I have a new riddle for you," he said. Pete smiled. Mr. Parcel set his mailbag down in the nearest booth. "What's the only day of the week that doesn't end with the letter *y*?"

Pete and Penny both stopped to think. "But they all end in *y*," Penny whined after a minute. "Monday, Tuesday, Wednesday, Thursday, Friday, Saturday, Sunday!"

Pete frowned and tugged on his lower lip. Then his eyes lit up. "The actual *days* do," he agreed. "And yesterday and today end in *y*, too. But *tomorrow* doesn't!"

Mr. Parcel smiled. "Bravo, Pete!"

"That was a great one," Pete told him. "Thanks!"

"We have to run," Penny said, tugging on Pete's arm. Mr. Parcel nodded. "Mom, Mr. Parcel's here!" Penny called out. Then she led Pete out the door.

"Okay, where do we start?" Pete asked as they entered Tidy Tomes.

"I'm not sure," Penny replied. "Hey, wait a minute! How about over there?" She pointed to a section near the back. The sign above it read HOME & GARDEN—just like in the message.

Pete grinned. "Of course!" They ran over to the bookshelves.

"No running in the store, please!" Mr. Tome warned. Pete and Penny slowed down.

"But what are we looking for?" Pete wondered as they looked around. The Home & Garden section was full of books on gardening, home repair, and home decorating.

"I don't know," Penny admitted. "But this section must be what the message wanted us to find." She noticed Jake checking books in a nearby section. "Hi, Jake!" she called out.

Jake glanced up and smiled quickly. Then he looked over at his father. He went right back to the books. *Wow, he's shy*, Penny thought.

Pete and Penny searched the Home & Garden section. They looked in between books and even checked the shelves themselves. "I don't see anything here," Pete said finally.

"Me neither." Penny frowned. "We could ask Jake. Maybe he knows something."

"Good idea," her brother agreed.

Wee-oo! Wee-oo! Wee-oo! A loud siren suddenly filled the air.

"That's the fire alarm! File out of the store! Stay calm!" Mr. Tome shouted. He waved customers toward the door. *He doesn't seem calm,* thought Pete.

Pete and Penny left as quickly as they could.

"I don't see any smoke," Pete commented once they were outside.

"I don't, either," Penny agreed. "Maybe it was a false alarm. We get them in school sometimes." She sighed. "I don't think Mr. Tome is going to let anyone back in tonight, though. We might as well go home."

"Yeah," Pete said quietly. He shoved his hands in his pockets. "Man, I was really hoping we'd figure out something big!" Then he brightened. "But, hey, I bet Dad's got dinner ready for us by now."

That cheered Penny up, too. "Race you!"

They hurried home.

Chapter Four

"We still don't know what that message means," Pete said to his parents the next day. Pete and Penny had explained all about the brick and the riddles over their after-school snack. "We only know where it was pointing us. I guess we'll just have to watch that section of the store again tonight."

"Why?" Penny asked. "It's so boring!"

"I'm sure you'll figure it out," their mom said.

"You two *are* the town puzzle experts, after all," said Mr. Pizzarelli.

"For now, though, you can puzzle out a way to help clean up," their dad said as he walked into the kitchen.

"Okay," Pete said. He hopped up and put his empty plate in the sink. Then he went out into the restaurant to make sure everything was set for the dinner crowd to arrive. Penny was right behind him. She started refilling the straws.

Churr! Penny heard a strange grinding sound. "What was that?" she asked.

Pete stopped to listen. "It sounded like something scraping against—" he said.

Penny walked between the booths. "The brick!" she yelled. She pointed toward the wall they shared with the bookstore.

Pete and Penny looked at each other. They raced over to the wall and pulled out the loose brick. Sure enough, they saw another message in there. *A new clue!* thought Pete.

Pete and Penny studied the picture.

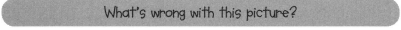

What's wrong with this picture?

(Answer, page 62.)

"These books are all in alphabetical order," Penny said after a second.

"Yes—except for the one with the elephant on the cover," Pete said. "This has to be about the bookstore again. Didn't Jake's dad say one of the books was in the wrong place yesterday?"

"So Jake put a book in the wrong place." Penny shook her head. "What's the big deal?"

"That's not the only problem the new bookstore has had lately," her brother said. "Remember, one of the bookcases collapsed yesterday. And the fire alarm went off. Maybe Jake is causing those bigger problems, too."

"But why would he? It's his dad's shop," said Penny.

"Maybe Jake doesn't want to help out in there. Maybe he didn't want to move to a new town. I don't know." Pete shrugged. "We don't know anything about him. The only things we know for sure are this new message has something to do with books being out of order and whoever left this message was just in the bookstore!"

Penny's eyes widened. They both raced for

the door. "We'll be next door for just a minute!"
they called out to their parents on the way.

They ran into Tidy Tomes. Mr. Tome was
behind the counter as usual. "No running in the
store," he scolded them.

Then they saw Jake. He was straightening the
books on a shelf in the Sports section. Penny
waved at him, but he quickly looked away. *Why
won't he talk to us?* she wondered.

Mr. Shears was there, too. "Well, hello,
kids," he said. He was bringing a book up to
the counter.

"*Code Breakers of Vietnam*?"
Pete read.

"That's right! It
reminds me of when I
was in the war," Mr.
Shears explained. "My
unit escorted a pair
of code breakers one
time. Hair-raising
stuff! In fact,
secret codes like
Morse code and the

Navajo language have helped us win wars!"

Pete and Penny looked at each other, mouths gaping. They were both thinking the same thing: *Code breakers? Morse code? Could Mr. Shears be the one leaving us messages?*

Just then, Mrs. Crier came into the shop. "Hello, children," she said, rubbing her shoulder. "Mr. Fields sure ran out of here in a hurry! Banged right into me, too! Probably going home to check on those vegetables of his! I swear he babies those plants worse than most parents!"

Penny frowned. *Why was Mr. Fields in such a rush? Could he have left the message?* she wondered.

"Ouch!" Mrs. Crier yelled. She'd just tripped. "Mr. Tome, you should really keep your shop more organized! You've got books lying all around the floor. It's dangerous!"

Mr. Tome leaned over the counter. Pete and Penny looked down as well. There was a large book on the floor: *Wonderful Watering Wisdom.*

"Jake!" Mr. Tome yelled. "What is this book doing here?"

"You'd better be careful," Mrs. Crier

warned. "If word gets out that people could hurt themselves here, you might have trouble getting any customers!"

"Jake!" Mr. Tome called out. A vein on his forehead was bulging.

"I think we'd better go," Penny whispered to Pete. He nodded and followed her out the door.

"Maybe Jake *is* the one doing things," Pete said as they walked home. "Sabotaging the bookstore could be a way to get back at his dad for yelling at him all the time."

"Maybe," Penny said. "But I'm still not convinced."

"Well, either way, this all has something to do with the order of the books," Pete said. "At least the new message told us that much."

"True," Penny agreed.

"We'll have to investigate this more tomorrow," Pete said.

"Hopefully tomorrow will be soon enough! We need to solve this mystery fast—before anyone gets seriously hurt!" Penny said. They both headed into the kitchen for dinner.

Chapter Five

Pete and Penny stopped by the bookstore on their way home from school on Thursday. They needed to figure out what was going on and who was causing all the problems. Both of them were itching to solve the mystery!

"No running," Mr. Tome told them.

"We're not," Penny pointed out. Mr. Tome raised his eyebrows at them.

The bookstore was quiet today. Only Mr. Fields, Benny, Ms. Green, and a couple of kids from school were there. Penny saw Jake reading in a corner. Even though he went to their school, Pete and Penny hadn't gotten to talk to him. And now he was probably supposed to be working. Penny pretended she hadn't seen him, thinking, *He deserves some time off!*

"Come on," she told Pete. She headed toward Home & Garden.

Pete pulled her back before they entered it. "Wait!" he whispered.

Ms. Green had just gone into the section. She seemed to be looking over her shoulder a lot for some reason. Pete and Penny hid behind a bookcase to watch her.

Ms. Green pulled a book off one of the top shelves. Penny saw the title: *Terrific Trimming Techniques*. Ms. Green flipped through the book for a second. She looked around quickly. Then she slipped it into the tote bag slung over her shoulder!

"She's stealing that book," Penny whispered. She started forward. But Pete stopped her.

"Let's watch to see if she does anything else," he suggested.

Ms. Green turned away from the bookcase. Pete and Penny moved back.

Ms. Green left the Home & Garden section. She walked over to Mystery & Thrillers. They crept a little closer. Ms. Green reached into her bag. She pulled out a different book! Then she looked around, set it on a shelf, and walked quickly out of the store.

"Maybe she's the person who's been sending us messages. Maybe she actually saw us just now and this is her way of leaving us a new clue," Pete said. "Something could be in that book!"

"Let's find out," said Penny. She grabbed the book Ms. Green had left in the Mystery & Thrillers section—*Growing Glossy Greens*. Penny carried it over to a couch in the corner of the store. Then she and Pete flipped through it.

Pete stopped on page 124: "Terrific Tomatoes."

"There's money in here!" A five-dollar bill had been stuck in the book.

"Maybe she was just using it as a bookmark." Penny had seen people use dollar bills that way before. But she didn't see anything interesting on that page. Or in the rest of the book, either. "It's all about trimming plants."

"And there aren't any puzzles." Pete frowned. "We should put it back where it belongs."

They took the book over to Home & Garden. They found the empty spot on the shelf with the rest of the *G* books. "There!" Penny said, placing the book back where it belonged.

Pete glanced at his watch. "We'd better go help Mom and Dad get ready for dinner."

Penny nodded. "I'll just hold on to the five dollars," she said as they left. "It is evidence, after all."

Pete rolled his eyes, but didn't say anything.

Pete and Penny returned to the bookstore after dinner. Ms. Green was there again—this time in the Self-Help section. Pete and Penny hid behind some books. They watched as she pulled *Terrific Trimming Techniques* from her bag. She looked around, quickly grabbed some books off a shelf, and started piling them on the floor. Then she climbed up on the pile and set *Terrific Trimming Techniques* on a high shelf—out of sight. She got down and went to pick up the books. Then Pete and Penny heard the front door open. Ms. Green jumped. She quickly walked over to the Home & Garden section. Pete and Penny followed. This time she picked up a book called *Caring for Cool Climbers*. She put that one in her bag as well!

Pete and Penny were confused. "I can't believe Ms. Green is stealing books!" Pete whispered as they walked to the front. "She's usually so nice!"

"She's not *really* stealing," Penny said. "I mean, it looks like she brings each book back, right?"

"She's still taking books without permission," Pete replied. "That's stealing."

"Should we tell Mr. Tome?" asked Penny. "Would he even believe us?"

"I'm not sure he'd listen to two kids," Pete said. "Just look how he talks to Jake. We need to find out more about what's going on here before we say anything. Besides, I like Ms. Green and we've known her awhile."

Just then Mr. Tome spotted them hiding behind the bookcase. "What are you two up to over there?" he demanded.

"Nothing, Mr. Tome." Penny gave him her best smile and walked over to him.

"Did your father get my order for tomorrow's grand opening event?" Mr. Tome asked.

"Yes," Penny replied. This time her smile was real. "You'll have the best pizza in town!"

"*Oof!*" Mr. Fields grunted from across the store. Mr. Tome raced over. Pete and Penny followed him. Mr. Fields was stumbling away from a bookcase in the Self-Help section. "I just tripped over these books in the middle of the floor," he said. He pointed to the pile Ms. Green had made to reach the high shelf. "I could've gotten seriously hurt!"

"I'm so sorry, Mr. Fields," Mr. Tome told him. "I can't imagine how those books got there."

Then Mr. Tome turned to Pete and Penny. "Did you two do that?" he asked them. "I did see you over here a minute ago."

"No," Pete said. "We didn't put books there, honest!" He and Penny headed to the door.

"Maybe I should have bought this place after all!" they overheard Mr. Fields telling Mr. Shears.

"It's a good thing you weren't hurt," Mr. Shears said. "I'd hate for you to miss the Tastiest Tomato competition this weekend! Have you seen the banner Ms. Green has up for it?"

Pete and Penny scooted out of the bookstore. *Will Jake get blamed for this accident, too? Then again, was it an accident?* wondered Pete. *If enough people start avoiding the bookstore, Mr. Tome would have to close it down. Then Mr. Fields could buy it instead!*

"Hey, Pizzarellis!" two voices called out.

"Hi, Elliot and Rupert!" Pete shouted back.

"We were on our way to Pizzarelli's for dinner," Rupert Jest said. "We made something for you!" He handed Pete a piece of paper.

"A rebus!" Pete exclaimed. "The pictures form words." He held out the page to Penny.

(Answer, page 62.)

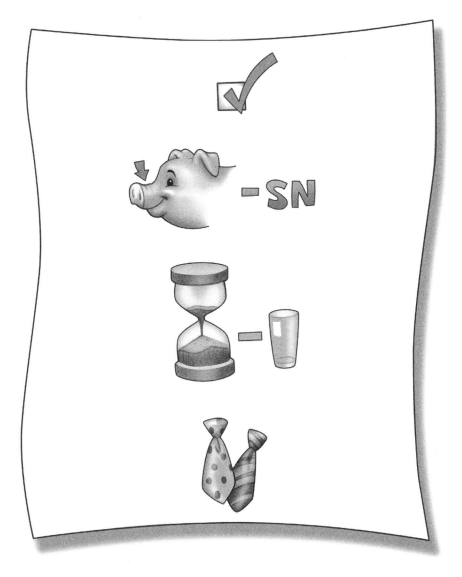

"What's that?" Pete asked, pointing at the first picture.

"It looks like a check mark," Penny answered.

Pete grinned. "Right—I mean, check. And that arrow is pointing to the pig's nose. That must be snout!"

"And *snout* minus *sn* would leave *out*," Penny continued. "Check out!"

Pete nodded. "An *hourglass* minus *glass* is *hour*," he continued. "And that last picture of two neckties"—Pete snapped his fingers—"must be just ties!"

"Check out our ties!" Penny stated.

"Exactly!" Elliot and Rupert beamed. Then they tugged on their ties—and the ties started flashing and playing music.

"The TieBall!" cheered Pete and Penny. The Jests had entered a toy contest, but another toy-store owner had stolen their design. Pete and Penny helped the Jests catch the thief. And their toy design won the contest!

"The TieBall goes on sale this weekend," Elliot explained as he handed Penny a box. "So we brought you one."

"That's great! Thanks!" said Penny. She and Pete already had one TieBall—the Jests had given them the original prototype as a thank-you. But now they could each have one.

Rupert grinned. "After you," he said, holding open the pizza parlor door and bowing to Pete and Penny. They laughed as the Jests ushered them inside. Still, Penny couldn't help wishing they could figure out what was going on with the bookstore as easily as they had solved the rebus from the Jests.

Chapter Six

"What's going on out here?" Pete asked Mrs. Crier the next morning. Pete and Penny were just about to leave for school. A crowd was gathered in front of the bookstore.

"Take a look," Mrs. Crier said. She pointed at the bookstore's large, front window.

Pete and Penny pushed their way to the front. The books in the window weren't in neat stacks today. Instead, they were displayed in a row across the bottom of the window. And the books on the display bookshelf were spine-out instead of face-out like usual. They weren't in alphabetical order, either. Everyone could see Mr. Tome through the window—scolding Jake.

"Mr. Tome is furious with his son," Mrs. Crier told them. "It must've been Jake's doing— no one else had access to the window overnight. Mr. Tome had apparently created an elaborate window display before going to bed last night. Now he'll have to completely redo it in time for tonight's grand opening celebration!"

Pete and Penny stood back from the crowd.

"Why would Jake rearrange the books like that?" Penny asked Pete.

"Maybe it's a message," Pete said.

They both stared at the books. They could see Mr. Tome yelling at Jake inside the store. "Maybe the colors of the spines mean something," Penny suggested. "Look! All the books on that bookshelf are either blue or yellow. Maybe blue means one thing and yellow means something else?"

Pete laughed. "That's it! It's Morse code again!" he told Penny. "The blue books must be the dashes and the yellow ones are the dots!"

Penny smiled. Pete quickly pulled out his notebook and started to copy down the message. Just in time, too! Mr. Tome was starting to scoop the books up to rearrange them.

Bang! A loud crash came from inside the store. A second later, Mr. Shears stumbled out holding his head.

Pete glanced up. He quickly finished copying down the code.

Decode the message. (Use the secret code in the front of this book!)

(Answer, page 62.)

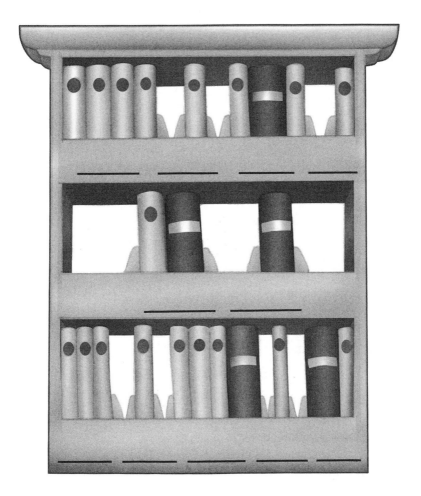

Pete and Penny rushed over to the barber. "Are you okay?" they asked at once.

"I saw a book I wanted that was up on the shelf," Mr. Shears explained. "I tried to pull it out, but it was stuck. So I gave it a good yank." He rubbed at his head. "The whole shelf of books exploded onto me! One of the books hit me on the head!" He pointed, rubbing the bump.

"You're not bleeding," Penny told him. "But you should put some ice on it." She and Pete walked Mr. Shears into the pizza parlor. Mrs. Pizzarelli rushed out from behind the counter.

"I swear, it's like that store is cursed," Mr. Shears muttered. "All these accidents! It's a wonder no one's been seriously hurt yet!"

"All this trouble could be the end of Tidy Tomes," Mrs. Pizzarelli agreed. She handed Mr. Shears an ice pack. "It's really too bad. I like having a bookstore for a neighbor!"

I like it, too, Penny thought as she and Pete headed to school. But their mom was right. The bookstore might be forced to close before it even opened—unless Pete and Penny could figure out what was going on and put a stop to it!

Chapter Seven

Pete and Penny went to Tidy Tomes after dinner that night. It was almost seven o'clock—the time noted in the window's Morse code message.

The bookstore was full of people. It was the grand opening! Everybody was there—Benny, the Jests, Ms. Green, Mr. Fields, Mrs. Crier, Steve, Mr. Shears, and even Ms. Scoop. She was a reporter for the *Redville Gazette*. She had written articles about Pete and Penny before. There were

TV reporters and a film crew from the local news at the event, too. Balloons and streamers coated the ceiling. The balloons all had pictures of books on them!

"Look, there's Jake! He's over by his dad at the register." Penny pointed. Jake and Mr. Tome were behind the counter together. Both of them were wearing ties.

Jake's face lit up when he saw Pete and Penny. He looked over at his dad working the register beside him. Then he suddenly nodded at Pete and Penny. Jake took a book off the counter, then set it back down but kept his hand on it. He started tapping the cover. Pete watched Jake's fingers. He was tapping quickly sometimes and slowly other times. He kept nodding at Pete and Penny as though he wanted them to understand something. Then Pete got it.

"Jake sent the messages! And he's tapping a message to us right now in Morse code!" Pete told his sister. "That's how it works—the long taps are dashes and the short ones are dots!"

"What's he saying?" asked Penny excitedly.

Pete pulled out his notebook. "Let's puzzle it

out!" He copied down the code Jake was tapping
out. Then he translated it into letters.

Decode the message. (Use the secret code in the front of this book!)

(Answer, page 62.)

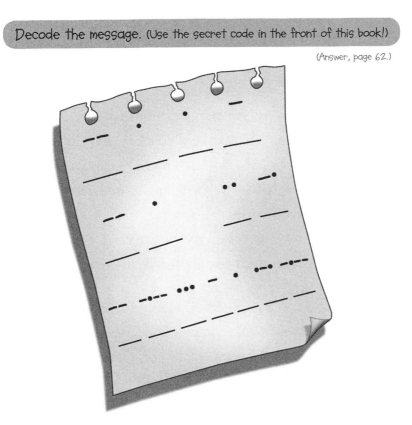

"Maybe we'll finally find out what this is all
about!" Penny said. She dragged Pete after her.

Jake met them in the Mystery & Thrillers section
a moment later. "You understood my messages!" It
was the first time they'd heard him speak.

"We did," Penny agreed. "And obviously you found out how much we love codes. Why didn't you just talk to us, though?"

Jake hung his head. "I was embarrassed. But I'd read about your puzzle-solving skills. I thought if I left you puzzles you could help me."

"We're happy to help," Pete told him. "You're worried about all the store's problems, right?"

Jake nodded. "My dad thinks all the problems have been my fault. But I didn't cause any of those things to happen! I swear!"

"We believe you," Penny promised. "I actually think we may have an idea who did."

"Well, we *do* know who's been moving books out of order," Pete corrected.

"Really?" Jake shook his head. "Who?"

"Ms. Green—the tall woman over there. It seems like she's been, sort of, borrowing books," Penny explained. "She takes one and then brings it back. She puts it in the first place she can find before anyone can notice what she's doing."

"But what about everything else?" Jake asked. "The shelves and the stacks and the fire alarm? Did she cause all those things, too?"

"Only one way to find out," said Pete. Ms. Green was standing near the counter, talking to Benny and Ms. Scoop. "Let's go talk to her."

"We'll do the talking," Penny assured Jake.

He led the way toward the counter. Penny ran to grab *Terrific Trimming Techniques. Maybe I can prove what Ms. Green did with it,* she thought.

Ms. Green saw the boys heading toward her. Then she saw Penny with the book. Ms. Green's eyes got wide. She rushed toward the door.

"After her!" Penny shouted. All three kids ran across the room.

"No running in the store!" Mr. Tome yelled.

But this time they ignored him.

"We know what you've been doing," Penny announced.

"I don't know what you mean," Ms. Green said. Her tote bag slipped off her shoulder. A book fell out of it!

Pete snatched it from the floor before she had a chance to hide it. Pete read the title out loud: *"Perfecting Plants."*

"Aha!" cried Penny. "The bookstore burglar has struck again!"

"Oh my!" said Ms. Green. All eyes were on her. She let out a sigh and fell to the floor!

Chapter Eight

"Let me through!" Mr. Fields shouted. He pushed his way to the front of the crowd. "I know first aid!"

He reached Ms. Green's side. He checked her pulse. "She's fine," he announced. "She just fainted." Someone brought him a glass of water. He cradled Ms. Green's head in his arm and sprinkled drops on her face. She blinked.

"Give her room," Mr. Fields said. He helped her sit up.

"What is going on over here?" Mr. Tome demanded, coming to stand beside Mr. Fields. "Ms. Green, are you okay? Why was that book in your bag?" Ms. Green looked over at Pete.

"She's been taking books," Pete told Mr. Tome.

"But I wasn't stealing them," Ms. Green insisted. "I was only borrowing them. I always brought them back!"

"You were putting them back in the wrong places, though," Penny pointed out. "And dangerous things have been happening—all because of those misplaced books."

"The collapsed bookcase?" Mr. Tome asked. Jake nodded. So did Pete and Penny. "Ms. Green shoved a book onto that already-full bookcase? That must be why it collapsed! And the firemen said the fire alarm went off because the furnace overheated. They found a pile of books covering one of the heating vents. Ms. Green left that pile there?" Penny nodded.

"She must have set up that book that hit Mr. Shears, too," Pete added. He looked over and saw Mr. Shears touch the Band-Aid on his head. "And she most likely left the one on the floor that Mrs. Crier tripped over." Mrs. Crier rubbed her foot, even though Pete was sure it didn't hurt anymore.

"Do you mean all those terrible things were my fault?" Ms. Green wrung her hands. "I'm so sorry! I didn't think borrowing books would hurt anyone! I didn't mean to hurt your store, either . . . I did leave *some* money each time!"

"That is true." Penny reached into her pocket. "We found this five-dollar bill in one of the books." She gave Mr. Tome the money.

"And I found money in a book when I was alphabetizing," Jake admitted. He looked down at the floor as he spoke.

"This is not a library, Ms. Green. We *sell* books," Mr. Tome said. "You own your own shop—you must understand." He shook his head.

Ms. Green hung her head. "I know it seems silly, but I didn't want anyone to see what I was reading. I couldn't admit that I needed those books. And really, I've already used up the library's gardening selection," she said.

"Wait a minute," Pete said. "Was this all about that tomato competition? We found your dollar bill marking a page about growing tomatoes."

"Yes. You see, I was trying to prepare for this weekend's Tastiest Tomato competition. I had to make sure my veggies were the best they could be—because of all the pressure to be the best vegetable grower in town! I need people to respect me as a gardener so they'll keep buying fruits and vegetables from my shop."

Mr. Fields picked up *Perfecting Plants*. "I thought this book looked helpful, too," he said. He pulled the same book out of his bag. "I just bought a copy, in fact."

Ms. Green stared. "You've been reading up on growing tomatoes, too?" she asked. "I thought you'd laugh if you knew I was turning to books for help."

Now Mr. Fields *was* laughing. "Are you kidding? I've been buying gardening books all week! My whole life really. Like I tell my students, you can learn a lot from a good book!"

"Come to think of it, Mr. Fields, you were always around when Ms. Green was here—we saw you. When she saw you, she'd just stick the

books wherever she could and leave as quickly as possible," Pete said slowly. He was puzzling out the mystery. "You're the reason why Ms. Green didn't put the books back in the right section." Pete guessed, looking from Mr. Fields to Ms. Green.

Ms. Green nodded. "I was embarrassed. I'm really sorry," she said. She was as red as a prize-winning tomato.

"Ms. Green never realized all the problems she was causing because she'd already left the store by the time something bad happened," Penny added. "While it wasn't right of her to take the books, she didn't know she'd caused such dangerous situations."

Ms. Green turned to face Mr. Tome. "I'm sorry, Mr. Tome. If I'm still welcome here, I'd like to purchase *Perfecting Plants* now," she said.

Mr. Tome smiled broadly. "Of course. But next time, stick with the local library for all your book-*borrowing* needs."

Jake smiled. He was standing beside his father. Mr. Tome placed a hand on Jake's shoulder. "I'm sorry I didn't believe you, son.

You're always a good helper. I should have known you wouldn't be that careless with the books."

"It's okay. I made a couple friends this way," said Jake. He smiled at Pete and Penny. Then Mr. Tome walked to the register with Ms. Green.

"Jake, your messages are what helped us solve the mystery, and together we caught the thief," Penny said, smiling.

"And *I* got a great, new story," Ms. Scoop called out from the crowd. She laughed. "Leave it to you two to solve another mystery! This will be great publicity for the bookstore!"

"Ms. Scoop, will there be a crossword puzzle with this article—like with the others?" Penny asked after she and Pete finished telling her the whole story.

Ms. Scoop smiled. "I already have it written! What do you think?"

"I'd say this calls for some pizza!" Pete said.

"Did somebody say pizza?" Mr. Pizzarelli called out as he came into the bookstore. Mrs. Pizzarelli was right behind him. They were

Use the clues to solve the puzzle.

(Answer, page 62.)

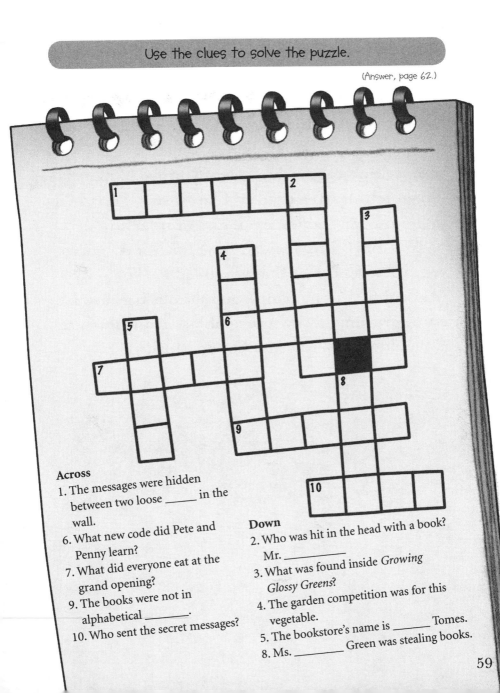

Across

1. The messages were hidden between two loose _____ in the wall.
6. What new code did Pete and Penny learn?
7. What did everyone eat at the grand opening?
9. The books were not in alphabetical _____.
10. Who sent the secret messages?

Down

2. Who was hit in the head with a book? Mr. _____
3. What was found inside *Growing Glossy Greens*?
4. The garden competition was for this vegetable.
5. The bookstore's name is _____ Tomes.
8. Ms. _____ Green was stealing books.

carrying several large pizza pies. "Food for the grand opening!"

Pete and Penny told their parents about what had happened while they set out the pizzas.

"Good luck at the Tastiest Tomato competition tomorrow," Penny heard Ms. Green telling Mr. Fields. "I know you'll do well—your vegetables are always wonderful."

"Thanks," Mr. Fields replied. "Good luck to you, too, Vera. Not that you need it. The only reason I don't buy from your shop is because I enjoy growing my own vegetables. Your produce always looks lovely." Ms. Green blushed.

Penny smiled. "May the best tomato win!" she said to both of them. They laughed.

"I'm so glad we nabbed our burglar!" Penny said to her brother. "Not only are Ms. Green and Mr. Fields getting along well now, but this bookstore is going to be great!"

Jake came over to them. "You know what else is great?" he asked. He had a slice of pizza in his hand. "This!" He took a big bite.

"We're going to be good friends!" Penny said, laughing. She took a bite of her own slice.

Pete was too busy eating to say anything. He just smiled—with a mouth full of pizza.

Answer Page

Page 3

Page 13

GJOE
UIF
TFDSFU
JO
ZPVS
XBMM

Find the secret in your wall

Page 21

Keep an eye on
Home and Garden

Page 28

Page 40

= SN

Check out our ties

Page 45

Here at seven

Page 49

Meet me in Mystery

Page 59

B R I C K S
H
E T M
A O R S E O
T S N
P I Z Z A S E
T I A Y
D S V
Y O R D E R
R
J A K E

OKANAGAN REGIONAL LIBRARY
3 3132 03310 0035